Stella Rousaki was born and raised in the island of Crete. She has a bachelor's degree in Biomedical Sciences (class of 2011) and a master's degree in Neoplasmatic diseases (Medicine school, 2015). She then studied acting at the Vasilis Diamandopoulos Drama School in Athens (class of 2018). She also studied acting on camera with the internationally renowned director Pandelis Voulgaris and attended acting seminars with Andreas Manolikakis, Eleni Scotti, and others. She participated as an actress in six stage plays and had a guest role on a Greek television series. She has written five stage plays and a script for a short movie, candidate for local and international film festivals. Her first writing attempt was the stage play *White Reality* which performed in Athens in 2018. She then wrote *The Spectacle of Time* (2020) which is a play based on the life of American author, Tennessee Williams, and has not been yet published. In 2022, she wrote the play *When the Clock Stops Ticking* which was chosen to partake in 'off-off' Theatre Festival of Athens.

To my mother, Vasileia, and my grandmother, Styliani,
who never stop believing in my own reality.

Stella Rousaki

WHITE REALITY

AUSTIN MACAULEY PUBLISHERS™
LONDON • CAMBRIDGE • NEW YORK • SHARJAH

Ordering Information
Quantity sales: Special discounts are available on quantity purchases by corporations, associations, and others. For details, contact the publisher at the address below.

Publisher's Cataloging-in-Publication data
Rousaki, Stella
White Reality

ISBN 9798889109532 (Paperback)
ISBN 9798889109549 (Hardback)
ISBN 9798889109556 (ePub e-book)

Library of Congress Control Number: 2023922833

www.austinmacauley.com/us

First Published 2024
Austin Macauley Publishers LLC
40 Wall Street, 33rd Floor, Suite 3302
New York, NY 10005
USA

mail-usa@austinmacauley.com
+1 (646) 5125767

Thanks to the actors of the stage play which inspired this novel, and the people who gave this piece of work its first 'spirituality' and shape:

Spiros Katsianos, Vivian Svolimi, George Boukaouris, Stelios Hatzigeorgiou, Theodora Vana, Georgia Aggelou, Panos Koulis, Panos Bakandreas, George Vasilopoulos and Maria Solomou, George Giannimpas, Semina Papalexandropoulou, Anastasia Dekavalla, Dimitris Karamanos, Froso Korrou and Dimitris Kouroubalis.

Special thanks and praises to Danae Stamatopoulos, who translated this novel into English and imprinted the image of my soul through the words.

Thanks to Vasiliki Kappa who did the editing for the transfer of the play into a novel and to the artist Andreas Pavlou, who helped me with the idea of the cover.

Table of Contents

White Reality

"Perhaps life is best described as a bad dream, between two arisings."

Eugene O'Neil

The Preparation

The space contained a naked lamp hanging from the ceiling and a table. The table had nothing but empty drinking glasses on it and it was surrounded by identical chairs. Next to the space was another, warmer one, like a small living room. It contained two small armchairs dressed in floral covers in earthly colors, a little bar, and a floor lamp. The two spaces seemed to belong to different worlds, separated by two windows with no curtains, kind of like separation lines.

The rest of the space was dark and oddly big, as if there was 'more of it' hidden in the dark. There was a spot across the rooms where one could see two small white armchairs standing alone. They had nothing to do with the rest of the space as if they had been there forever. There was no clock, and the atmosphere created by the warmth of the lamps was that of an old, underlit home.

A woman, well-dressed and around thirty-five, walked into the space joyfully and decisively. She held a folder. She sat on a chair across the rooms and studied the folder carefully. She seemed sweet and mature despite her young age. Her hair was brown, and her eyes deep blue. She checked her watch, the only thing that could give her a sense of time.

After a while, two women walked into the space and sat on the white armchairs. Blanche was tall and delicate. She wore a red dress from a different era, which seemed threadbare from use and the passage of time. Her hair was blonde and shoulder-length. It was obvious that she tried to hide the fact that she hadn't been combing it quite scholastically. She wore heels – also red – with discreet yellow flowers on them. She looked like a princess, a forgotten princess, although she knew very well that she remained one. The other woman, Mary, was a little older. She wore a light burgundy dress that left her white neck exposed as it fell on her petite frame. On her neck, you could clearly see her golden cross. Her hair was blonde, similarly combed as Blanche's, with the only difference being that she had tried to arrange a ballerina bun. Her hands had a strange liveliness that did not obey the rules of gravity. It was as if they were trying to leave the body and form the most beautiful ballet pose. The two women sat next to each other on the white armchairs.

Surely, under the semi-darkness, one could easily confuse the two figures. In light, however, their small differences, those that made them two separate entities, were apparent. They stared at the two rooms mechanically. They did this every day. It seemed as if they expected that one of these days, something unique would happen.

Yunis, the woman holding the light blue folder, smiled and looked at them in a calming manner. She avoided interrupting the inner monologue they seemed to be having. After a while, she looked at her watch and closed the envelope. She entered the small living room of one of the two half-lit spaces. Edmond, a young man, was sitting there. He was pale and puzzled, pretending to read a book. He looked like a child anticipating to get his homework done and go play. Next to him stood the bar with the empty bottles. Yunis quietly walked towards the bar and filled the bottles with water. Edmond gave her a few quick glances and continued reading.

"Where is my mother?" Edmond effortlessly asked as if that was the only word he kept inside him for hours.

"In the guest room! She's not asleep; she's just resting. She says she has a terrible headache," answered Yunis.

Yunis left the room, leaving young Edmond even more skeptical. He jumped at the chance of secretly grabbing a drink. His attempt was cut short by his older brother Jamie, who entered the room about to tease him.

"Why in secret rascal? You can't fool me; you're a worse actor than I am!"

Jamie was condemned to accept the path his father, James, had planned for him. He dreamt his son would one day become a successful actor as he once was. He believed his strong network and knowledge regarding the field would always be a powerful asset for his son to take on the career that was ingloriously cut short for him.

Jamie provocatively denied the path his father had carved out for him. He was always an unpredictable rebel, a man of himself who never kept his mouth shut, always trying to escape all that tormented him since childhood. He was neurotic and restless, contrary to his brother Edmond, who seemed as if he always stood on a cloud or in moving sand. He considered nothing to be stable and took nothing for granted. His eyes had a constant fog, like the fog his mother, Mary, adored.

"Listen, sport, you know me. I never tried lecturing you, but the doctor's right. You need to cut down on the darned alcohol," Jamie said.

"Well, starting today, once the news comes out, I'll quit. I know I'm sick, but I don't think it's something serious," Edmond replied casually.

The two brothers always looked for a topic for discussion before their father came home for dinner. The usual void hour before dinner, during which the two brothers found the chance to talk about women and work while drinking and laughing mechanically, always careful to not consume the whisky bottle that their father would measure. Their talk froze abruptly for a few seconds, during which they ended up looking around the space, searching for a presence. The first word came from Jamie's bold mouth.

"Where's Mom?"

"Upstairs."

"What time did she go upstairs?"

"A while ago, she said she was going to lay down."

"Why didn't you tell me?"

"Tell you what? She was tired and went to take a nap…she didn't get any sleep all night."

"Was she alone in the morning? Haven't you seen her at all today?"

"No, I was here reading…"

"Is she coming for dinner?"

"Of course."

"Of course, what's that supposed to mean? Maybe she's not hungry. Or maybe she'll start eating by herself upstairs. It's happened before…" Jamie said.

"She accused us of spying on her, that's why I didn't check up on her and, actually, she's not quite wrong…she gave me her word, don't worry!" said Edmond, trying to keep his voice, which had started to tremble, down.

"So? She's given her word before. I don't recall her keeping it!" said Jamie, trying to contain the stream of thoughts that had flooded his mouth and was about to burst. Doubt, which always protected him from destruction, as well as his brother's poor health since he suffered from tuberculosis, held him from speaking any further about the matter.

"Sorry, I'm late. I ran into the neighbors. You know, they never stop once they start talking…" James, the two boys' father, interrupted while heading straight to the bar to measure the bottle.

James Tyron was a man around sixty-five. He had the proud gaze and stout carriage of a great actor of his time. Fate and life forced him to step out of his artistic garment in order to survive economically. However, from time to time, he anxiously tried to put it back on for his audience.

"Don't bother measuring! Not a single drop less than how you left it!" Jamie said.

"That's not why I was looking at it; I know your tricks! Why such a dark atmosphere? What's going on? What's with your faces?" James replied.

"Rest assured, yours won't be any better," Jamie answered sarcastically.

"Shut up!" Edmond replied, trying to avoid the conversation about to follow. James always knew where the conversation would lead, so he looked for Yunis, the housekeeper, to serve dinner as a way out. He was afraid that at any minute, words he did not want to hear would be spoken, so he diplomatically led his sons to change the subject and get on with the 'practical' part of the day!

Mary watched the scene from her white armchair, noticing every small detail. Her gaze had started to leave the space. It focused on each face as if she was examining a rare painting, trying to penetrate their very souls, searching for something she could never find until then, something she desperately avoided while 'upstairs' in the guestroom.

Yunis entered the space containing the table and empty glasses. She switched on the light, a warm yellow light stemming from the naked lamp. She filled two glasses with water and left a deck of cards on the table. There were two men sitting there. Stanley and Mitch. They were smoking, laughing, and playing cards.

Stanley was a man around thirty-five with a rough face and imposing features. The sound of his voice was intense, like a siren, and one could hardly make sense of his words, especially when he shouted. His body was muscular and strong, while his hands seemed to have a personality of their own, almost as if they were constantly ready to shoot a gun. Mitch was something like Stanley's alter ego. He was the same age but of a subdued and kind disposition, although his gigantic figure pointed out the opposite. The two men often hung out to play poker during the hours they didn't work at the factory.

During the game, a cheerful jazz melody started to play. Yunis accompanied by a woman entered ceremonially carrying a chest. The two men carried on playing without seeing or hearing what was going on.

Blanche watched the two women from her white armchair. Her eyes focused on the chest as if it was the most important item in the space. Mary looked at it in the same intense way. The other woman was Stella Kowalski, Blanche's younger sister and Stanley's wife. A young woman around thirty-five with expressive eyes and long black hair in a simple ponytail. Her body was lively, dynamic, and earthly, but everything about her was sloppy and carefree, contrary to her sister's appearance.

"What'd you tell her?" Yunis asked Stella, carefully placing the chest on the floor.

"I told her we arranged for her to go on a trip and rest. She's really confused. I don't know if what I did was right...I could never carry on living with Stanley had I believed her story..." Stella answered.

"Tell her she's pretty, Stella..." said Yunis.

Yunis quickly departed, and Stella was left staring at the chest. The two men finished the game and left quickly and carelessly, leaving a mess behind them as they always did after a few rounds of poker. Stella mechanically went to tidy up the space and upped the volume on the small radio from which the jazz music was playing.

It seemed like poker nights were something she was well acquainted with, a loud habit of her husband's that didn't seem to bother her at all. On the contrary, she seemed to enjoy it. Her torrential and free spirit was the exact opposite of her sister's. So opposite that it seemed as if the two of them came from completely different worlds.

Blanche looked at Stella with a sweetness that wasn't so pure. It seemed to hide bitterness and disappointment inside it. It was the first time she got up from the white armchair and slowly approached her sister. Her walk was abstract and unstable, and she ended up exactly under the lamp. Her figure seemed like a shadow in the underlit room.

"Blanche!" Stella exclaimed.

"Stella, can you please explain to me what exactly you're doing in a place like this? It's like my worst nightmare! And…this…this noise…it feels like I'm stuck in a forest full of vampires!" said Blanche.

"It's not that bad here, Blanche…I think you're exaggerating!" Stella replied, laughing. "How about a drink?"

"Just a glass!" Blanche abruptly answered and started gulping the drink Stella gave her.

"You haven't commented on my look!"

"You're so beautiful, Blanche!" Stella replied almost automatically and very enthusiastically.

"You see. I'm really vain when it comes to my appearance…even now that it's deteriorating and…abandoning me," Blanche said.

Stella interrupted Blanche, wanting to change the subject, which would surely agitate her sister.

"That's not true, Blanche, you're beautiful! Have you met Stanley?"

Blanche noticed Stella's awkwardness, took on her words, and continued at her own pace.

"I noticed him…not very bright, may I say! I'd really like to know what you think is so special about him!" Blanche said mockingly.

Stella's face lit up. She started describing Stanley to Blanche through her eyes. She walked up and down the room almost as if she was flying, although her walk remained on earth. Blanche remained frozen under the light; her feet seemed to be screwed to the floor. She made no reaction to Stella's quick movement, and her gaze left the space as if she was dreaming.

Stella abruptly stopped talking. She studied Blanche for a bit, realizing that her sister had been lost in her thoughts. In an attempt to bring her back to reality, she turned off the music. Blanche slowly walked to her white armchair.

"Blanche! Where are you going?" Stella tried to stop her.

"To wash my face," Blanche abstractly replied, nodding to Yunis, who was watching her.

Yunis switched off the light and switched on the floor lamp in the other room. James Tyron was there with a glass of whiskey in hand. He seemed absent-minded, lost in his thoughts. Yunis approached Mary, who was sitting on her white armchair, and urged her to go to James. She got up, slowly and unstably, as if her shoes were much bigger than her small feet. She very discreetly went near him and placed her hand on his shoulder to wake him up.

As she touched him, her hand came to life as if it didn't belong to the rest of her body. Mary's hands were thin and fragile, making it obvious that she once was a great pianist because only then would those hands be so nervous and lyrical. James jumped at her touch as if he was seeing her for the first time.

"You know what I noticed, Mary? Now that you've gained some weight, you fit perfectly in my arms!" he awkwardly told her and took her in his arms.

"You mean I gained too much weight! Not everyone has your stomach! I've been eating too much…and I really need to order new glasses; my eyes are not helping at all!" Mary replied.

"Your eyes are lovely, and you know it! I think someone is fishing for compliments! I look at you and admire how strong, healthy, and beautiful you look! Do you know how happy it makes me to see you gain your health back? That's why I want you to take care of yourself, do you understand?" James said in an awkwardly enthusiastic way, trying to hide his agony.

He was always a very good diplomat, especially when it came to his wife's vanity about her looks. He knew very well how to create a different reality from that which she saw in the mirror.

"Edmond hasn't had any breakfast…just coffee…he always says he's not hungry. The truth is summer flu always cuts down one's appetite, but I'm not worried. He'll be okay if he's a little careful…" Mary answered, speaking to herself.

While she was talking, James looked at her in the eye, carefully thinking of how he would avoid the subject he wished wouldn't be brought up.

"Did you hear the siren last night? It kept me up! You haven't gotten any sleep either, right? I heard you tossing and turning all night!" he told her, smiling forcefully and strangely.

Mary realized he was trying to change the subject and insisted on bringing up Edmond again. She glanced at Yunis as if waiting for her to give her a sign for her next word. "Why don't you finish the fence together? It'll do him good to sweat a little; it's healthy to sweat! But don't waste time; you need to do it before the fog…it'll be foggy soon…I can tell by the rheumatisms on my hands…they are the perfect weather forecast!"

As she was talking to herself, she abstractedly left James and walked to her white armchair. He watched her go, trying to make sure everything was okay, and he hadn't said anything to upset her. Yunis got up from her chair and put on a piano melody, Mary's favorite. She quickly calmed down, and James switched off the light.

There's a time when you have to go, even if there's no certain place for you to be.

Tennessee Williams

The First Truth

The piano melody Mary loved continued to play in the other room. The atmosphere was sweet, like summer dusk. Stella decorated the place like for a celebration. She was abstractly dancing to the music and doing her usual dinner preparations, only this time, it was for her sister's birthday. She never knew how many candles to put on the cake because Blanche never revealed her age. She chose to put a single, symbolic candle so as to not disappoint her.

Blanche, sitting on her white armchair, looked at her and smiled gently. She seemed to know very well what her sister was thinking. Stanley, having just finished at the factory, entered the room with his usual heavy walk and indifferent gaze. He saw the set table, balloons, and a cake.

"What's the occasion?" he asked Stella, obviously not caring about her answer.

"Blanche's birthday!" Stella replied enthusiastically.

Once he heard that, Stanley's disposition changed; he seemed uneasy, as if he had seen something unwanted in his house.

"Blanche's birthday! Right. And? Where is she now?"

"She's having a hot bath to calm her nerves! She's really upset. She went through absolute hell…you see, we lost our estate, the big house with the white columns I showed you in the pictures…it had to be sacrificed; there was no other way! And Blanche…well…she hadn't expected we'd be living in a house like this…I used to sugar coat things for her when we talked, so…"

As Stella spoke with her unpretentious naivete, Stanley tried to hold back a huge and overwhelming stream of thoughts. It seemed that he was about to explode with just a touch. Blanche paid full attention to Stanley; she was trying to figure out what her sister could have said that bothered him so much. Fear had paralyzed her, and she desperately tried to arrange her hands and legs on the white armchair she was sitting on. She searched for help in Yunis' gaze, who was, this time, in greater agony. She tried to hide it by giving a reassuring glance to Blanche.

"You lost the estate…did she show you any papers? A contract? Anything? How the hell did you lose it?"

"Stop it! She'll hear you! I don't think it was sold. She hasn't shown me any papers; I don't care about the papers!"

The words that came out of Stella's mouth were the very words Stanley didn't want to hear. Unable to hold his anger, he started sweating and turning red. Like a wild animal desperately trying to break free from its cage. Blanche's gaze became deeper, scared and about to betray her sadness. Yunis made no attempt to stop the dialogue. She continued to carefully monitor Blanche's feelings as if trying to make her keep her eyes shut in front of a horror film they were watching together.

"Let me get some things straight here. Where I come from, what belongs to the wife belongs to the husband and vice versa. I'll wait for her majesty to explain to me what's going on! I think you've been fooled, baby. And if you've been fooled, I've been fooled. And I won't put up with that. Are we clear?" Stanley said.

His body, out of control, moved to the chest, which he violently opened.

"And what about all this stuff in here? How'd she buy it? With her teacher's salary? Open your eyes, Stella! Look! Fur coats, gold dresses, fox fur…where's your fur baby?"

Each item Stanley threw out of the chest seemed like a bullet passing in front of Blanche's eyes, making her shed tears that landed on her dress. The chest Stanley emptied out seemed to her like her very self. Each and every bit of hope keeping her to life being ripped apart. Stella abruptly shut the chest and answered with childish anger, as if she hadn't really realized what Stanley's anger had done to Blanche's psyche.

"Please close the chest before she gets out of the bathroom. And give her a break. Tell her something nice. Try to understand and be kind to her…say something nice about her dress and her looks; those things really matter to Blanche. She's very sensitive, Stanley, more than the usual…she's been raised in a much different way than you have."

Blanche's eyes were filled with tears of sadness and love towards her sister's words. The space in front of her became blurry and damp. Everything was obscure, almost as if she was dreaming. Yunis made no attempt to stop the action taking place and left Blanche to completely lose herself in the image in front of her.

"Your sister is lying in your face; do you know that? I managed to dig up some information, which, of course, didn't surprise me at all. I made sure they were true and even had the evidence to prove it! So, lie number one: All those stories about how the only man who ever laid hands on her is the doctor who gave birth to her…Sister Blanche is not that innocent after all. The factory supplier knows everything about this town. He lives in a hotel where the lady often finds herself and knows her far too well! She's quite notorious there, a third-category hotel from which she was kicked out, needless to tell you why…"

Blanche's hands shook like a fish out of water. She desperately tried to fit them under her knees and squeezed them with all the strength she could muster. Yunis started leaving her spot in agony, trying to find a way to stay put on the chair.

"The thing about lady Blanche is that she couldn't wander around town any longer. Once someone her true colors were revealed to someone, they'd leave her. She'd find someone else to serve her pretty lies to. Unfortunately for her, the town is small, and nothing stays secret for long. That's how your beloved sister became the crazy girl of the town and came to us…so this is princess Blanche's upbringing…and now to lie number three…"

Stella was frozen, listening to Stanley, anxious that Blanche might hear what he was saying from the bathroom. The bathroom was Blanche's safe place when the 'truth' about her was unfolded outside of it. Stella was either well aware of that truth or had come to realize it but didn't want to accept it. She tried to juggle her passion for Stanley and a mandatory tenderness towards her sister.

"Lie number three…do you really think she's going back to work? No, baby! She wouldn't dare go back there.

She was kicked out, and the reason why makes me wanna puke…she hooked up with a seventeen-year-old boy!"

Stanley's phrase echoed in Blanche's ears. She immediately erased Stella's presence from her blurry eyes. Now, only she, Stanley, and his words were present in the half-lit room. It was almost as if there was someone else there, a shouting monster that struck her, making her body lose its balance and wobble.

In the other space, Jamie turned on the light. He was holding a glass of water. His hands were nervous. His father stood across from him. The tension between them matched the one between Stella and Stanley as if they were all in the same room. Mary, sitting in her white armchair, looked at them with a sweet bitterness. Her agony concentrated in her nervous, thin hands, which she constantly rubbed as if she were looking for something that would give her an answer to all she tried to comprehend. Yunis turned the page on her folder and now focused on the father and son.

"What'd the doctor say? He's sick, right? Damn it! We wouldn't be here had you taken him to a real doctor," Jamie said, lighting a cigarette with a nervousness he had taken after his mother.

"Why? What's wrong with the doctor? It was always the same doctor," James said.

"He's a con artist. He's just cheap. Had Edmond been a piece of land, you'd sell your soul to buy him! That's what you did with Mother, and look at us now."

James filled the glass with water and drank intensely. His son was used to show him a reality that he knew very well but avoided seeing. Money was the only principle managing his thoughts. Life seemed to owe him something, even if it was to remind him that it's never too late to have another look at reality.

"That doctor has known Edmond since he was a baby. But what can he do if Edmond leads that sort of life? "James replied in an attempt to apologize to his son. "He might be stuck in bed for years, and it's such a shame…he had made such a good start and found a job that suits him…it's a shame about your mother, too…it tears me apart to see her pining away for him when she should be resting…you have no idea how pleased I was to see her near us again, strong and sure of herself! She held her anger, but now she seems scared and nervous. She mustn't find out the truth, but I'm afraid we can't avoid it! The worst part is, her father died of the same disease, she can't forget that, she adored him…"

"Yes, Father. She really seemed to be in great shape," Jamie replied with careless cynicism.

"She was in great shape! What do you mean she 'seemed' to be? What's on your mind?"

"Nothing, it's just that last night, around three, I woke up and heard her walking up and down the guest room. And then in the bathroom…I pretended to be asleep but heard her. For a moment, she stopped in the middle of the corridor and tried to hear if I was asleep…we all know that when she locks herself up in that room, it's a sign that…"

"No sign! No mystery! My snoring was bothering her; where'd you expect her to go? How the hell can you live with a mind that constantly thinks of the worst? Edmond's illness is like a curse for her; he got sick once she gave birth to him, and that was the first time…"

"How is it her fault? Why are you accusing her?"

"I'm not!"

"Then who are you accusing? Edmond for getting sick? Who are you accusing?"

"Stop it! She'll hear you! She's still walking…God knows when she'll go to sleep…" James interrupted without wanting to hear another word about what he already knew. Jamie was for him, the voice he couldn't have himself, the conscience that tormented him ever since his son started to grasp the way the world works. Mary had stood up from the white armchair, but her feet were nailed to the floor, leaving her unable to approach the room any further. It was almost as if her eyes had a will to leave her body in an attempt to approach the others. Before Mary's next step, Yunis switched off the light. She then took a candle and placed it on the cake in the other room for Blanche's birthday.

God gave us eyes that seal and ears that don't. That should tell us something.

Eugene O'Neil

The Shadows

Stella looked at the cake with admiration, proud of what she had prepared for her sister's birthday. She set the table and placed the plates and cutlery. On the center of the table was the cake with the candle Yunis had placed. Stanley sat on the chair, dressed in a white t-shirt and dirty pants from the factory. He held a cigarette from which each draw held a thought of how he could destroy the party that had been prepared for Blanche. He smiled ironically and decided to speak once he put out the cigarette.

"Just one candle?"

"Always…for Blanche."

"Are we expecting company?"

"I've invited Mitch. The two of them are really close. Blanche would love it for him to be here…"

"I don't think you should be expecting him. He's not coming. Mitch is my friend; I told him everything about her. He doesn't want to see her ever again!"

"No! He can't find out the truth!" Stella interrupted him in agony.

Blanche stared at the candle. She searched for a light that would give her an explanation about what came out of Stanley's words. Stella indifferently carried on checking if everything was ready, trying to think of an excuse to tell her sister about Mitch's absence.

"Oh! I forgot to tell you I have a gift for her! A bus ticket! I couldn't possibly come by empty-handed!" Stanley said sarcastically, smiling at Stella.

Blanche suddenly shut her ears as if she had just heard the intense sound of the bus that passed by her sister's house. 'Streetcar named Desire', as they called it in the neighborhood, always made a noise as if it was ready to collapse.

Yunis noticed Blanche trying to shut her ears with all her strength and decided to stop the conversation between Stella and Stanley by going to the other room.

The two brothers, Edmond and Jamie, were there. This time, both of them seemed to be drunk. Jamie always tended to be more intense and provocative, while Edmond was melancholic and puzzled.

"That's right! Turn on the light, will you? That cheapskate likes keeping you in the dark, huh?" Jamie said.

"You're wasted, stop drinking, you'll collapse!" his brother replied, knowing that was a useless piece of information for Jamie.

"What's our stoned daisy up to? She asleep?" Jamie yelled.

"Keep your voice down!" Edmond said in a desperate attempt for his mother not to hear.

Jamie's words struck Mary's ears, who was sitting on the white armchair, just like the sound of the bus struck Blanche's. She mustered her panic in her hands, which seemed to be trying to detach themselves from her body and tenderly and apologetically caress her sons' heads. Her fingers twitched and unwrapped themselves from each other, giving the impression they would reach the boys' heads from a distance.

Jamie, full of despair and hopelessness, placed his hands on his face as if he had felt Mary's touch from afar. He stood there for a while, crouched down and silent. Mary rose from the armchair, but Yunis' gaze communicated to her that it wasn't time yet…

"She fooled me. She said she wouldn't start her addiction again and I believed her…I'll never forgive her! Do you know what that meant to me? I thought that maybe if she'd change, I'd start changing as well…you see, I knew long before you did…I'll never forget the first time I found out…then your disease came along. That was the final strike! I know what you all think of me, but do you have any idea how much I admire and how proud I am of you? Why wouldn't I be? I created you! You're my Frankenstein! Who taught you to hide and not make mistakes? Who urged you to read poetry? And please, don't worry about going to the hospital. You'll be just fine in six months' time. In fact, you might not be that sick, really; those doctors have no clue…"

"Let's drink!" Edmond said, realizing that his brother's delirium would never stop if he didn't manage to convince him that everything was okay. Edmond had to try and juggle the pity he felt for his brother and father as well as the hope he had for his mother. His task was to juggle between craving and death, something he had only read in books and poetry until then. Books and poetry were his escape mechanism away from the home he lived in.

"Listen, little one. We might not get another chance to talk about this, so you need to take it seriously. Father and Mother are right. I'm a bad influence! And what's worse, I'm doing it on purpose."

"Stop it, Jamie! I don't want to hear it!"

"No, you have to! Part of me desires to destroy you. It's the part that's been dead for years and despises life. I used to dread your success. I was jealous of you since the day you were born. I pretended my flaws to be virtues in front of you so that you wouldn't exceed me. I even knew that had you never been born, Mother wouldn't start…no, that's not what I meant to say…I love you, little one, I really do…but you need to protect yourself from me…I hate myself, and I'm willing to take revenge from anyone I can! Especially from you, first chance I get, I'll stab you in the back! And I might even like the fact Mother started again, you know why? I don't want to be the only corpse inside this house."

Edmond interrupted his brother's outburst, slapping him on the face and throwing him on the floor. The slap galvanized Mary's body, which started floating between the white entrance room and the half-lit room her sons were in. Yunis approached her, gently touched her frail hands, and led her back to her seat in an attempt to make her feel safe.

"That's it…I feel much better now…I know you've forgiven me, kid…you're a smart boy…take care of yourself…may God keep you safe!"

At that moment, their father entered the room, as he always did after the small chat he always had with the neighbors before dinner. He noticed his son, Jamie, on the floor, dazed from alcohol and redeemed from his confession. He looked at him with disgust and despair.

"What a disgrace! My firstborn! Supposed to carry on my legacy with honor and dignity! A flabbergasted bum!"

"Father! Our very own Othello! Where could our Ophelia be? She shooting up again?"

"Shut your mouth, Jamie!" Edmond cried in despair.

"Punk! You don't give a damn about your own mother! I'll kick you out of here!" James yelled.

Jamie, suddenly snapping out of the drunkenness of his body and mind, got up and looked at the two men with despair and sadness. His voice started to change. Knowing he laid out all his cards, he had nothing to hide. He spoke in a stout and warm voice.

"You think I feel no pity? I pity her more than any of you do! I was the one who found her with the syringe in hand! I only thought hookers took drugs until then. I know she's going through an inner battle...I'm not insensitive...I'm just upfront about what we all know but have no courage to admit! But we'll have to go through it again...no therapy can save her. All it can do is temporarily fix the problem. Having any hope would be pure madness!"

"Don't talk like that! I want to have hope...have you ever prayed for her? She just started; she might be able to stop if she manages to discipline herself...I'll go talk to her," Edmond said, trying to reassure himself.

"You'll be wasting your words...she won't listen to you...she'll be here presently absent...she'll drift away from us until..." James bitterly apologized, having exhausted any attempt to not admit the truth to his sons.

Mary stared at Edmond as if he was the only light, she could lay her eyes on. As she heard his words, she grabbed the cross on her neck. She seemed to be praying in her head as she continued to stare at him intensely.

Yunis entered the room and interrupted the conversation.

"Dinner is ready! It'll get cold, and you'll be yelling at me!"

The men left the space as if signaled to do so. Stella switched on the light in the other room.

She mechanically checked if everything was ready for her sister's birthday party, and Stanley watched her, smoking ironically. Every cigarette he pulled out of the pack was like a threat to Blanche. The conversation continued at the same pace, giving Stella a pleasant sense of liveliness that made her forget what a threat Stanley was to Blanche.

Blanche, sitting on her white armchair, anxiously tried to arrange her hair, placing on it a faux tiara she had with her. It was her favorite accessory, which she only wore on special occasions. She was granted a gaze of admiration from Yunis, whom she smiled to, sadly confirming she would never stop caring about her appearance, which was the only identity she could keep forever.

"Mitch will be here, Stanley. Blanche invited him for her birthday, and he'll be here, right?"

"I told you, he's my friend. I told him the truth about your sister, baby! That she's older than she claims…you see, she never dared show herself to him in light…that she's not as noble as she pretends and that she chugs my drinks in the bathroom! She's got a problem, Stella. He asked around town and found out the whole truth about her! Your beloved sister has lied to him about everything…and of course, when she realized she has nothing left, she asked him to marry her!"

"Marry her? What did he say?"

"He said she's not 'clean enough for him to take to his mother', ragefully putting out his last cigarette and sardonically kissing Stella. She remained frozen under the small lamp, hiding the light from the balloons and ribbons, making them appear as shadows about to confirm her sister's demise. At that moment, as if she were a shadow herself, she looked at Yunis like a child whose party had been ruined. She then glanced at her sister, who was sitting on the white armchair, hoping that Blanche would realize the truth. She and Yunis started talking in a conspirational manner, like when the two of them were talking on the chest."

"Where's Blanche?" Stella asked.

"In the bathroom," Yunis replied. "What will you tell her?"

"That we've arranged for her to go to the countryside to get some rest. I'm so confused; I don't know if what I did was right…I won't be able to go on living with Stanley if I don't believe his story…"

"Life must go forward. No matter what, we need to go on our path," Yunis said.

Stella turned off the light and stood there, a blurry figure staring at the cake with a single candle on it.

In the other room, one could notice a masculine figure. James was sitting on the armchair. There was an eerie silence, similar to that before a storm when everything was calm and secret. Edmond, his son, entered the room. He looked around him, probably trying to figure out if the only presence was that of his father's, and poured himself a drink. "She's upstairs, can't you hear?" James said, recognizing Edmond's agony.

"When did she go?" Edmond asked.

"Once you left, she lost her appetite. Where were you? Why'd you leave, son? Did anything happen?"

"I was wandering in the fog…I love the fog, Father…if only you knew how much I need it. That fog was where I wanted it, waiting for me. I walked for a while and then turned back, and the house wasn't there anymore. Almost as if it never existed! I felt so calm. I was a ghost within a ghost…she's also a ghost…wandering around us like a shadow living in the past while we're sitting here pretending to forget, stretching out ears nonetheless to hear the slightest noise. Everything is heard in the silence, like irregular strikes of a damaged clock…back when I wasn't even born yet…"

"You fool! Fog doesn't do you good! And what's all this nonsense you're talking about? Why are you accusing yourself? You keep reproducing your mother's nonsense…" James said abstractly.

"We're searching in vain! It's all your fault! You and your darned stinginess! None of this would have happened had you taken her to a good doctor! When did you ever give her any joy? You didn't even build her a proper home! All you did was drag her to cheap hotels and abandon her when you went on tour. And then you came back all drunk! She was raised differently, Father…very differently…you're just a disgusting cheapskate! That's what you are! Just thinking about all that makes me wanna puke! I despise you!"

Edmond noticed his father's sad expression. Immediately, his gaze was filled with guilt and pity.

James was frozen as if he had just woken up from a dream. The two of them stood there, silent, trying to comprehend the truths that came out of Edmond's mouth. Mary watched her beloved son and felt touched and relieved. He had just told his father everything she longed to tell her husband all these years. The sadness in his eyes, however, was mirrored in hers, which became foggy and wet once again…

"I may be a disgusting cheapskate, as you say, but I've fought and suffered in my life! You always had everything! I was just a kid when my father abandoned my mother. She was left behind, having to raise four children on her own. I was very ambitious, Edmond! I wanted her to be proud of me…I'd read every single stage play I could lay my hands on and had the greatest actor of my time as an audience when I played Othello for the first time! That was the most crucial part of my career, and I had the ambition to go further. That's when I married your mother and entered the path of easy success and certainty! Life led me where it wanted and, in the end…His words about my delivery are on a piece of paper…I saved it somewhere and read it from time to time. But, in the end, it did me harm, and I didn't want to lay eyes on it anymore! I wonder where I put it actually," James mumbled, trying to connect his words with lines of an entire lifetime.

"It should be in the chest with Mother's wedding gown...Isn't that the last bus?" his son mechanically replied, avoiding talking about everything he truly hid in his heart about his father.

"Well, if it isn't for your daft brother. Let's wait for him; I don't want to go upstairs while she's awake," James said. Edmond nodded with a 'yes', signifying an informal agreement for them to not go upstairs while she was awake in the bedroom. Once she heard that phrase, Mary shut her eyes, trying to avoid the image of her beloved son, who carelessly gave up his mother's truth.

Yunis shut the folder she constantly held and turned on a light next to her. A blue, velvet armchair with a high back, which no one could see until then, appeared. She nodded to Blanche to sit near her. Blanche asked Yunis for permission to light a cigarette. It was granted. She then sat on the blue armchair. The smoke in the underlit room created a dreamy, foggy atmosphere in which Blanche felt safe and secure. She remained silent for a while, leaving Yunis' gaze to transmit to her what she needed at the moment.

"Yunis, do you like my cigarette case?" Blanche said with admiration, holding a shiny cigarette case embroidered with little white stones and an artistic stamp in the middle.

"Look, it has a dedication: Life is full of memories, except for the present moment, passing right in front of your eyes. Isn't it beautiful? It's a gift from a young, strange, and sweet young man who fell sick and knew he was about to die."

"He must have really loved you. Sick people tend to dedicate themselves wholeheartedly; pain makes us real.

The most beautiful things in life were made by those who truly suffered."

"I believe that too, Yunis. Show me a person who hasn't suffered, and I'll prove to you he's empty!" Blanche said.

Yunis let her smoke the cigarette she took out of the cigarette case for a while. She tried to find the words and time to talk to her through the foggy atmosphere that had been created.

"Blanche, I know how this all seems to you. People do not always act as they should. They sometimes do things they don't even understand themselves. That's real life. Stella really loves you, but there are things that happen between a man and a woman in the dark that make everything else seem pointless."

"That's beastly desire! Like that bus making that horrible sound, like a siren. We may not be in the image and likeness of God, Yunis, but things like poetry, music, and art have brought a new light to this world."

"Desire, like the name of that bus, Blanche…Have you ever been on that bus?"

"Yes, Yunis, that's what brought me here. I once loved someone I lost…He was a young, beautiful boy with something off about him. A strange tenderness with no animosity whatsoever. I loved him; I hadn't realized anything until after our wedding."

"Realize what, Blanche?"

"I had failed. I knew there was nothing I could do to save him or myself. I wasn't worthy of keeping him, Yunis. I knew something bad was about to happen, and it did."

Yunis let Blanche lose herself in her memories, not wanting to interrupt, even for a second, her train of thought and feelings overwhelming her. It was as if the smoke from her cigarette had led Blanche to a dreamy path of salvation. The 'present moment, passing right in front of your eyes', as written on her cigarette case, had been lost completely.

"We were on a trip. We stayed in that hotel room; I can't quite remember. The room wasn't empty; two people were there. The boy I had married and a friend of his, an older man. I saw them! We acted as if nothing had happened and went to the club. We laughed and drank on our way there until suddenly, the boy ran out. After a while, a gunshot! I ran out; his head was blown up further away…it was all my fault…my own fault. While we were dancing, I said, 'I saw you; you disgust me.' And then, the beacon that lit the world was off, and no light ever lit for me stronger than this one here. After Allan's death, I felt like I didn't belong. Loneliness…Do you know how everyone looked at me? A mixture of rage and pity, they turned their backs on me and stopped talking to me…My youth was suddenly swooped by a whirlpool. And then, all those deaths…I went through all those deaths, Yunis. Parents, relatives whose breath roared in your ears…funerals are beautiful. Full of flowers, serene…only if you spend the night next to someone's deathbed, hearing them say 'hold me' can you see the ugliness of death…I experienced all of it…the opposite of desire, death…and then I met Mitch. He was a small crack in the rock of the world in which I could hide. Serenity…serenity is heaven for the poor…but it seems I've asked for too much from God…"

"Death is one moment. Life has so many…hell is our own self, and the only way out is to put ourselves aside and face reality…not our personal reality, Blanche, the one outside our skin, outside our eternal incarceration."

We're all condemned to live in eternal incarceration inside our very own skin.

Eugene O'Neil

The Dinner

Yunis quietly left Blanche and turned on the light in the room she had prepared for her birthday. She tried to discreetly show her that the time had come to face Stella and Stanley in the present moment when everything became real. Stella and Stanley were already seated.

Yunis brought a huge plate of chicken and a plate of French fries, which she placed in front of Stanley. There were scattered beer bottles and glasses, and the cake was placed in the center of the table. Blanche, seated in the blue armchair, watched the festive table her sister had prepared while Stanley vulgarly ate and drank without caring about who was there. Blanche watched him with disgust and fear, looking for a chance to make her presence apparent in a way that wouldn't cause discomfort.

"Stanley, tell us a joke or one of those fancy stories you know!" Blanche said.

"I had no idea you dig my stories, Blanche. My stories don't fit your delicate taste!" Stanley replied indifferently, continuing to provocatively chew and gulp beer from the bottle in front of him.

"Mr. Kowalski is busy stuffing his face like a little pig. He has no time for anything else!" Stella answered in an attempt to calm the tense atmosphere that had been created in front of her.

"That's right! Absolutely right!" Stanley said sarcastically.

Blanche decided to get up from the blue armchair and sat on the wooden chair that was waiting for her.

"Did anyone call me?" asked Blanche in agony.

"Who, Blanche?" answered Stella, almost fearful from her sister's abrupt expression.

"Sep! The millionaire I met. I invited him here. I wrote: 'Dear Sep. My sister and I are in a desperate state.' He'll surely call me! It's my birthday, after all! Mitch came by. He brought me flowers and asked me to forgive him, but some things are unforgivable! I said, 'Thank you, but it was so stupid of me to think we could fit together. Our way of life is so different. Let's be real!'"

Stanley looked at her full of irony, gulping big chunks of food and trying to keep his mouth busy. At some point, he abruptly dropped the last bite from his dirty hand and decided to speak.

"Lies! Mitch never came back with flowers and the works, and I know it because I know exactly where he is, and frankly, he wants to have nothing to do with you!"

Suddenly, a strange silence occurred for a few seconds, which left Blanche feeling exposed. Her gaze penetrated that of Yunis' who was now very near her, and once she felt secure, she tried to continue celebrating her birthday. She knew that the day a person is born is bright and happy and that 'the present moment, passing right in front of her eyes', was her own birthday, and nothing should be able to cause her darkness and sadness. The candle on the cake may have been the light she was searching for.

"He was here though! He came by in his work clothes and repeated all the slanders he heard from you…but that doesn't matter anymore. Sep respects me because he's a gentleman and knows how to treat a lady! Really, Stanley, what sign are you? I bet you're an Aries…Arians love noise! They love to scatter things all over the place!"

"Stan was born five minutes before Christmas!" Stella answered, eagerly trying to hide the red cloth Blanche held for Stanley.

"Capricorn then! Or should I say, a goat?" Blanche said mockingly.

"What sign are you?" Stanley asked, looking for a word that would destroy the feast in no time.

"I'm a Virgo…you should have known…it's my birthday!" Blanche cheerfully continued, gulping down the drink in front of her.

"That's true…I should have known you're a virgin…sorry, a Virgo…that's why you like gentlemen, and of course, the attraction is mutual! I should have also known that you're full of lies! That you're only here because you got kicked out from the royal hotels in which you met gentlemen and even young boys occasionally…that you're only here because you have nowhere to hide and that you drink my booze in the bathroom like a queen! Let me tell you something, lady Blanche, I'm the king here! I'm in charge here, and as long as I'm around, you're nothing. Got it?"

Blanche suddenly got up from the chair and stood under the lamp. She shut her eyes as if blinded by the light, trying to find another white light within her, which would help her reach her own reality. Yunis approached her, like a beast tamer approaches a wild beast, and whispered in her ear.

"Carried away by a dream, you waste your life searching for a magic door, a lost kingdom of serenity…open your eyes, Blanche."

She moved away as if she woke up from a nightmare and met her sister.

"Stella! Turn off that light! Let's make some magic. Light up that little candle. Actually, no. Don't light it, Stella! Keep it for your baby's birthday. I hope candles light its whole life. Its aunt knows very well that candles don't last long. They blow away from our sight, the wind blows them off, and then electric lamps, like those in hospitals, go on, and then everything is crude, very crude."

"Such lovely poetry!" Stanley replied sarcastically. Blanche remained frozen, holding Stanley's present. Every warm and bright color had left her sight as if, suddenly…absolute darkness was there. She left the room at a slow, interrupted pace, her blurry gaze focusing on Yunis. Only the sound of her heels, drawn with flowers, was heard.

She sat on the white armchair, but her look was now distorted and faded, as if all that remained was her figure, a hologram of a white memory, just like the white armchair.

The seat next to her was empty. Mary had gotten up and was now in the next-door room. She stood there, alone, near the big window that made her silhouette seem even more nervous and frail. She sounded as if she was praying like the nuns had taught her before she met James. Yunis approached her, discreetly and silently declaring her presence, and sat on the other chair, waiting for her to speak.

"Do you like the fog, Yunis?" she asked her, signifying that she was ready. "I really like it…it hides you from the world…and yourself. No one can find or touch you. You're here, and you aren't. I wish it was always like this. Like this foggy night. Everything is wrapped in a dreamy veil. Nothing's real…magic…that's what I want, Yunis. To be alone in a world where the truth is not real, and life hides from itself. As if I'm walking under the sea, like a ghost of the fog."

Yunis watched her carefully and let her make a fantastical journey through the foggy atmosphere she had created in her mind. It was the atmosphere that made everything seem dreamy, as if her life hid behind masks. She decided to say the phrase that would bring her back to the moment, to the Tyron family's room.

"You'll be alone in a while, Mary…they'll be back. Food is ready. You need to get something to eat."

"I'm not hungry, Yunis. But I'll sit at the table to get this over with."

"Does the medicine…ruin your appetite?"

"It's a painkiller! You go back to the past…you only remember moments of true happiness; it doesn't only kill hand pain, you won't believe it, these hands were once musician hands! You know what I'm thinking? One day, I'll look in the mirror, pleased that time went by so fast!"

"Life is an isolation cell, Mary…with mirrors for walls."

"Silly romanticism! Girlish dreams! What's so special about a silly little student meeting a theatre idol? I was much happier before I found out about his existence…before my father took me to his dressing room. That was the first time I saw him. I fell in love, Yunis! I had no idea he was a drunk! I wouldn't have married him if I knew! I remember being left alone and afraid for hours in those dirty hotel rooms…that's when everything was gone for me, Yunis. It was all my fault."

"Why was it your fault, Mary?"

"One of the first sights our son Jamie had when he came into this world was his father drinking! Alcohol was never scarce from the table. I can't recognize my son anymore. He was a happy and strong child who never cried. Same with Eugene. That's how the two years of his life were until he died from my carelessness. Edmond was the only one to be a hassle when he was little. Always scared and anxious. I guess he was born scared. Probably because I was afraid to bring him into this world."

Yunis approached her and held her hand. She placed her on the floral armchair and calmed her down.

"Tell me about the child you lost, Mary…Eugene."

"He was just a baby when I left him to follow James on his tour. I thought his older brother, Jamie, would look after him. That he'd be like a guardian angel, as he looked when he was little…I had no idea, Yunis. I couldn't imagine what he hid in his soul since he was a child…I left him, I abandoned him, I still haven't found out the truth, Yunis. All I know is that it's all my fault…my carelessness for all three children. Nobody's fault but mine…"

"No one can change what comes their way. Once we realize something and try to avoid it, something else has occurred. And then something else, and something else…until we end up parting from our own self whom we lose forever."

Yunis went away from her and left her in the room's 'cold' reality. She was about to sit on the chair across from her and left free space for James and Edmond to come in. The two of them looked at Mary for a while, almost frozen, and then approached her hesitantly as if meeting her for the first time, hoping to not hear a single word from her. Hoping her presence to be that of a ghost that cannot touch or talk to them. To hear her walk was enough for them as a reassurance that she existed.

Mary noticed they entered the room and nervously rose from the armchair. She started talking to them with an eerie enthusiasm, foretelling that this dinner would bring them face-to-face with a hard truth they refused to comprehend for a long time.

"Thank God you're back! Food won't be long. You're a little early; you're usually too late! James, would you like some whiskey? How about you, Edmond? Would you like some? Of course, you shouldn't be drinking, but a little glass of whiskey before dinner can't be too bad! Where's Jamie? Oh, what am I saying! Why would he be home if he had a penny in his pocket? I'm afraid we've lost Jamie for good, darling. We mustn't let him influence Edmond…That's how jealous he was of Eugene, remember? He'll never stop if he doesn't manage to drag Edmond into failure…who would have guessed Jamie would ridicule us?"

"Mary, that's enough! Please stop talking! Can't you forget already?" James desperately cried.

"Father, didn't you say to not mind her?" Edmond asked in agony.

James looked for a way out of what was about to occur. As usual, his choice was to go to the bar and have a drink. He realized the bottle was half empty and used that as an excuse to shift the focus of the conversation.

"What's this? Who drank this? Jamie wasn't here. I hope he didn't start drinking on top of everything!"

Yunis got up from the chair and entered the room.

"Ma'am offered me a drink. I was keeping her company while you were away, and she was here alone…and because I bought her that medicine for her rheumatisms…you know…the painkiller."

Once he heard that, Edmond snapped, pouring himself the little water that was left in the bottle.

"For the love of God, Mother! Do you want the whole world to know that you…?"

"Know what, Edmond? That I'm taking painkillers? I had no idea what pain meant before giving birth to you!"

"Don't listen to her, son…she's far away from us when she says this nonsense…why didn't you keep a little extra stash in your drawer? Some prescriptions for when in need…I hope you get enough this time! I wouldn't want us to experience that horrible night you ran around in your nightgown, yelling that you were going to jump in the sea again!"

"Yes, James…I will have enough this time. I hope I overdose one day. I wouldn't dare do it on purpose…Virgin Mary wouldn't forgive me."

"For the love of God, Mary! For the sake of your children and myself, can't you just stop now? Or at least try?"

"Try what, James? I don't understand! I feel so lonely here; I have nowhere to go, and this medicine helps me forget. I used to have so many friends who lived in beautiful homes, like my father's home. But then that scandal with that lover of yours came out, and everyone stopped talking to me. Oh, now that I remembered, I need to go back to the pharmacy and get some soap and face cream."

Suddenly, a bus sound. The room was filled with silence, like an omen that something bad was about to happen. The sound was deafening, like the siren Mary heard at night, leaving her awake and terrified. After a while, only Edmond's voice was heard, disappointed and resigned, contrary to the intense bus sound.

"It must be Jamie. He's back with the line bus."

The other room was still filled with balloons and ribbons from Blanche's birthday party.

Used tables and plates were on the table. Everything was useless now. Nothing resembled the festive atmosphere Stella had created. All that remained untouched was the birthday cake with the candle still lit. Blanche sat alone at the table. Her hair was messy, and her little crown had moved as if it knew it didn't belong there anymore.

Everything on and around her was deserted. Her blurry gaze was stuck on the candle. She remained lost in what she saw in the yellow flame. After a while, Stanley entered. As if nothing had changed in the room and as if Blanche never existed, he threw off his shoes and vulgarly started to drink water out of the bottle. He nodded for her to drink, and with a nod, she stopped his peculiar enthusiasm.

"Stanley, how's Stella? How's the baby? Did everything go well?"

"Everything's fine. I came to take a nap. It's just you and me tonight! I'll keep you company one last night, wouldn't want you to go away disappointed! Unless…if you've hidden anyone under the bed! Oh! Now that I mentioned 'hidden', let's see what you've got in that chest of yours! Let's see if there's any paperwork on fur coats!"

"Don't touch that! There's nothing in it!"

"Whoa! Here's something!"

"Don't touch them! You're contaminating them…now that you touched them, I'll have to burn everything!"

"Cut the crap, let me have a look…What the hell is it?"

"Poems…from a boy that's not here anymore…because of me…I hurt him. It's my treasure, and no one can touch it!"

"I don't care about that! I care about the estate! What happened to it? Is it mortgaged?"

Stanley violently started searching inside the chest, throwing out all of Blanche's valuables and leaving exposed everything she wanted to hide deep inside, everything that reminded her of mortgages and papers belonging to her dead relatives' estates. Everything that was hidden under poems, memories, beautiful ornaments, and 'desire' covering up death.

"Here, take them! Examine them! Documents, papers…Each paper is a bite of our forefathers' estate. Our fathers and brothers munched on it in their romantic escapades! Since all you care about is papers, you can take them, all yours! Learn them by heart for all I care!"

"I've got a lawyer. I'll have him examine them. That Sep of yours must really admire you! Is that why you're all dressed up? By the way, when did he call? How come none of us heard anything? Oh, don't bother answering. I know why! There was no phone call because there's no admirer. It's all a big fat fantasy! Look at you! You're a mess! You couldn't fool me even for a second! You're wearing that worn-out dress you rented from the thrift store and that fake tiara with glasses instead of diamonds. Harsh realism, Blanche! Why don't you turn on the light? I wanna see you loud and clear! You never spoke the truth. You lied to all of us! Heck, your own sister doesn't even believe you! She pretends to! Of course, Mitch doesn't either. Lies, lies inside and out! You were never clean straight!"

"The human heart is not straight. It's erratic, like a mountain track. I don't want reality. I want magic and try to give it to people. I might not be telling the truth, but what I'm saying should have been the truth! I never lied, Mr. Kowalski, not inside me, not in my heart!"

"What about my booze you chugged all summer? Didn't you lie about that either? I knew you were looking for them in the dark and made Stella serve you while you were having your calming hot baths. You're sick, Blanche. Would you like one now?"

Stanley approached her like a wild animal approaches its prey. Blanche's face turned pale; her eyes had a penetrating fear as if they were trying to grasp the "actual moment of fear and rejection passing right in front of her."

Suddenly, the room was filled with a dazzling light that lit up her face and erased everything.

Stanley was lost in the light, and she was left frozen, deep inside the bright lightning that had surrounded her. A young man, dressed in clean and bright clothing, like a guardian angel, entered the room and surrounded Blanche with his calm presence, relieving her from her fear and darkness. She was now calm and tried to figure out whether he was real or a creation of magic that she wanted to see.

"Who are you?" whispered Blanche, almost as if talking to herself.

"I'm here to…" the man replied in a reassuring manner.

"Right…I see…I'm not ready yet…what time is it?"

"It's almost midnight…"

"Is it really that late? It should have been dark…but this light…I feel so strange. Thank you, my dear prince! I bet you're very young! Are you a student? What do you study?"

"Nursing."

"And what's your name?"

"Eugene."

The young man delicately and politely held Blanche, as if holding a valuable ornament and placed her on the white armchair. Her body had now taken an upright position, remembering how it once used to be, resurrected in its old self. Yunis watched her, relieved and calm, and went towards the room where Mary and the Tyron family were.

As the light switched on, the deafening bus sound was heard. Jamie appeared alone and absent from the dinner. He noticed the tense atmosphere in the room. His drunken gaze fell upon his mother, who was nailed to the floral armchair as if her body had lost its center. Her body was nervous, moving downward in a constant attempt to lose itself from everyone's sight and disappear.

"Why are you looking at me like that?" asked Mary, trying to hide her face from the mirror her son had made for her.

"You know why…"

"No, I don't."

"You think you can fool me? I know you, Mother. Look at your eyes in the mirror; look at yourself!"

Yunis entered their conversation, trying to make what was created in front of Mary's eyes as painless as possible.

"Dinner's ready, Jamie…they're waiting for you…" she said and turned on the light in a 'hidden' room. One of those rooms that had not been yet revealed.

A big table set with plates and glasses, around which sat James and Edmond waiting for the Tyron family's usual dinner. They watched Mary and Jamie's encounter without participating, unwilling to ruin one of the usual days that made them delicately hide reality. Jamie quickly realized their signal and tried to find a way to get away from his mother.

"For the love of God, let's eat! I've been working all day; I deserve a plate of food!" he nervously said, leaving Mary behind. This was an excuse he knew would make her stop talking. She remained on the armchair, struck by her family's indifference and evasion, trying to find a way out of her sunken self. She looked at Yunis and decided to find the deep breath that would take her to the surface.

"It's nice we all get to eat together…we never had a real home…real homes don't make you feel deserted. I once had a real home and lost it…"

"This was once a real home, Mary. Before you…" James hesitantly replied, knowing very well that he was giving her the chance to tell him what she had been avoiding for a long time.

"Before I what? What did the doctor say about Edmond? Not that it really matters; it's just a cold…I know them. They do everything they can to humiliate you. They use you like a criminal; they don't take you for a human being. It was one of them that gave me the medicine for the first time. They sell your soul and yours to the devil, and you only realize it once you're in hell! I hate them!"

Edmond snapped and threw his fork. The sound of the falling fork reached Mary's ears like that of a siren, an omen that something bad was about to happen.

"Mother, for the love of God! You need to face reality! I'm sick! Whether you like it or not, I need to go to the hospital and into therapy!"

Mary's body rose from the chair in a way that seemed like she was in desperate need of help. Her eyes became shiny and lively; it seemed as if her tiny face was burning with fever. Her voice cracked in an attempt to declare that she wasn't a ghost living in the past. She was alive, constantly trying to reach their souls.

"I won't hear it! You're not going anywhere! I won't allow it! How can you allow it, James? No one asked for my permission; you're my child! I know why your father wants to lock you up in a hospital! He wants to take you away from me. It's happened before! He was jealous of you and made me abandon you…that's how Eugene died. It was my mistake! But I'm not leaving you now! Not this time! Do you hear me?"

Edmond looked at her with pity and replied in an angry outburst.

"I do hear you! Unfortunately! I can't do otherwise…but it's not very pleasant to know your mother is a morphine addict!"

Edmond's voice slowly dissolved from the room like the sound of the siren. They left a soft and blurry echo in Mary's head. She couldn't hear words anymore, and all that was left was a deafening beat right in the center of her heart. The white fog that made her hide now became a veil of desperation and resignment. She slowly rose from the floral armchair. All that was heard were her tiny footsteps.

"Can you hear the siren from the boats? Why does fog make everything sound so sad? I'm going upstairs to comb my hair…if, of course, I manage to find my glasses…you can come with me if you suspect I'm lying…for once, you can come with me…"

Jamie watched her. He was drunk and dizzy. His eyes refused to see her, and his ears couldn't hear her. He deliberately found the silent moment to dissolve the last hope that would make her return to the table.

"She's going to shoot up again!"

"Yes, Jamie. Seems I didn't take enough. My hands are in terrible pain…I can tell; I can tell from my hands. I better go get some rest…Bon appetite."

Jamie rose from his chair with a cry of truth and despair. He knew the moment that just passed in front of him was gone, and he made a vain attempt to return to his own reality. The one he could never reveal to the only person he should have for his salvation.

"Mother, I'm sorry, I'm desperate! Do you understand? You fooled me! You said you wouldn't start, and I believed you! You always accuse me of having the worst in mind, but I always try to think of the best…Have you any idea what you meant to me? I'll never forgive you!"

Mary disappeared from the room, Jamie's words echoing in her ears. At that moment, her firstborn cried out all that he had hidden since he was a child in his dark room. It was so dark, no crack from which a light could come in and warm up his empty soul. Her body suddenly seemed small, lost in her long dress, leaving exposed only her naked feet, which galvanized her to reach the white armchair.

As she moved away from the table where her family was seated, she seemed like a white memory inside the dark reality of the room. She sat next to Blanche, this time as if she was trying to reach her soul and search for what she had lost.

Candles don't last long…they blow away before our eyes…they blow away, and then electric lamps turn on, making you see the harsh reality.

Tennessee Williams

The Big Door

Yunis looked at the two women calmly and sympathetically after what had happened before their eyes. She remained silent for a while, then looked at her watch for the time signal signifying the continuation of their white journey. She seemed calm although in great agony. She opened the folder and noticed again the big table around which Mary's family was seated.

James was alone. His company was a glass of whiskey on the table. There was nothing else reminding us of the family's dinner. He was dizzy and lost in his blurry thoughts. His gaze was empty. It was as if he had thrown away all of his thoughts and was left with the company of his loneliness. After a while, Edmond walked in. He walked slowly and carelessly, free from all the weights that held down his body and soul. He looked at his father and started switching the light on and off, trying to snap both of them out of their lethargic attempt to 'forget'.

"Turn off the light! We're not having a party!" James said, agitated.

"It's just a little lamp. I almost tripped in the dark," Edmond soullessly replied.

"You'd see clearly if you weren't drunk."

"I'm drunk? Well, if it isn't for the pot calling the kettle black."

"Where's your brother? What am I saying? He'll come back and start drinking again. I hope he misses the last bus."

"Where is she?"

"Still walking up and down. She'll turn into a ghost again! Cheers! How about a game of poker tonight? I can't go upstairs while she's awake…" James suggested.

"Sure, why not."

James put a deck of cards on the table and filled his son's glass. The two of them had paused time at the moment they wished would stay forever. A moment in which reality was hidden by a veil of a forgotten memory and illusion, buried well within the room's semi-darkness.

After a while, the bus sound was heard. The two of them indifferently continued playing their game. Jamie's heavy footsteps were proof that he wasn't the only one lost in the vague conscience and mind freeze.

"Hello, boys! I'm drunk! I'm lit up like a kite! But I'm not flying; I'm still here! How's our stoned lady? Oh, I'm sorry…I shouldn't have…the alcohol, you see…why the hell are you looking at me again?" he said to his father, not caring to hear his response.

"I'm looking at what a loser you've become…" James replied unwilling to show any feeling of care towards his son.

The repeating 'game' scene of the three men now seemed eerie, detached from their consciousness. As if they had deeply buried all those words and images, they wished to hide but unwillingly came out at the family dinner. Mary stared at the table like she was watching a boring movie in the cinema. Nothing reminded her that those faces were her own family. All she saw were three strangers who portrayed a scene from her family life, which she had seen again and again before.

Her eyes had no sadness or disappointment…she was just an observer with no connection to the people across her. Blanche, still next to her, was listening to her own soul. She was reassured that nothing and no one could harm her. The two of them had obtained a third eye. An eye that viewed reality through a prism of a cold and neutral color. A color containing all colors, shades, and shadows. In the end, the only thing that would prevail, if they allowed it, would be a white light that would grant them the serenity they were looking for.

As the two women's energies 'connected', the Tyron family's table became 'bigger'. Stanley and Mitch, the uninvited visitors, entered the game silently. The sound of the cards and the rhythm of the game made them seem like blind players. Everything was governed by the bizarre rhythm of the card game, which was so finely tuned as if it had been practiced for years. Stella approached them and placed a candle, like that on Blanche's cake, on the table. She stood next to them, ceremonially glancing at the table and her sister's chest, which was still there. Her figure seemed vague and faded. So did the figures of the men who were obsessively lost in the game. The sound of the cards and poker chips was monotonous and intense. It seemed as if they used the game to push away any feeling or truth that could be revealed to them.

Yunis approached the two women and whispered in their ears.

"It's time…don't be afraid…this is the time that brought you here connecting your realities…step away from your guilt and fear and set them free as well…they are too imprisoned in their memories and harsh reality, in their eternal incarceration. Step away and set them free…"

Blanche held Mary's hand. The two women's bodies and souls connected. They took the same expression and became one, as their pasts connected. They knew that 'the moment passing right in front of them' was the moment their journey towards redemption had begun. They had found in the 'entrance room' what they couldn't find in the half-lit rooms of their homes. Through their own eyes, they saw neutrality, while in reality, it was like a blank piece of paper on which they could start writing from the beginning. They saw the only true reality existing in white color, allowing no shadows or other colors to distort it.

"This is the moment…the only true moment…step into the light!" Yunis said to the two women under the dry and abrupt rumbling of the game.

"Please, shut the curtains. I need to go outside!" Blanche said. She had said the same thing to Stella the day she would depart for the 'trip' Stanley and Stella had planned for her. She rose from the white armchair and walked towards the chest.

"My white dress…please check if it's ironed…I want to wear it! And my silver seahorse pin. It's here, in my chest…and…please find the bouquet with the fake violets…pin it on my dress…is the coast clear?"

"Yes, Blanche, you look wonderful…" Stella said, suddenly liven by Blanche's entrance.

"I washed my hair!"

"Really?"

"I don't know if I've rinsed them well."

"They look beautiful, Blanche."

Mary rose too and walked to the chest, holding a white dress. Jamie looked at her, continuing his intense playing; he said to her, "The madness scene! Enter Ophelia!"

"Has someone called me?" Blanche asked.

"Who, Blanche?" Stella indifferently replied.

"Sep…"

"Oh, right…no my love…"

"That's strange…I…" said Blanche.

James noticed the white wedding gown Mary was holding. The one she wore on their wedding and was well hidden in the chest. He entered the conversation without interrupting the game's rhythm. His words sounded like a percussion musical instrument in the two women's ears.

"What's she holding, Edmond?"

"Her wedding gown, Father…"

"Jesus! Mary! Give it to me, my darling! You'll step on it, and then you'll be inconsolable."

"Thank you! You're so kind…this is a wedding gown! Isn't it beautiful? I found it in the chest! I don't know what I needed it for…" Mary replied with an eerie voice, like the one she had the night she came out of her bedroom to find the men's silent game. To find the scenery of an estranged family that would push her away from them forever.

"I'm looking for something…" said Mary.

"It's no use, Father..." said Jamie, continuing to play and drink.

The two women's worlds had suddenly become one – a dark and violent world. Those familiar to them seemed to belong to the same family dragging along the heavy chains of their empty souls...The voices from the dinner table all sounded as one. Everything was tangled up, became soulless and similar, a dance of the undead under the beat of the deck of cards.

Yunis watched them, letting them influence each other. Her quiet gaze only tried to protect the two women, knowing that this was the last act of this psychodrama. In order to be redeemed, they would have to go through the path of their last memory intact.

"What's going on here? Why are you looking at me like that? Is something wrong with me?" Blanche said.

"You look beautiful, Blanche!" Stella replied. "What a lovely dress! Are you ready?"

Blanche and Mary completed each other's thoughts that ran like a stream. They were trying to find the magic 'door' that would lead them to the kingdom of serenity.

"Help me! Help me get ready!" Blanche exclaimed.

"My hands are swollen," Mary said, continuing Blanche's phrases.

"I can't wait to get out of here! This place is a trap!" Mary said, searching for Yunis.

"Listen! These bells are the only pure thing in this neighborhood...I'll go now; I'm ready," Blanche replied.

"She can't go yet!" Yunis said to Eugene, the young nurse, allowing for the two women's psychodrama to continue until the end and checking up on their emotional tension the way a doctor checks their patient's cardiograph.

"Mother, it's not a cold! I'm really sick!" Edmond cried, continuing to play like a cold executor.

The young nurse approached the two women, trying to calm them down.

"No! You can't stop me from going! It's not right! I spoke to the sister, she's so nice...Her blue eyes..." answered Mary to her son.

"Idiot! There's no cure!" Jamie added.

"I don't want to go through them," Blanche said.

"Then wait for the game to end," Yunis answered brashly.

"I can already smell the sea breeze...from now on, I want to spend the rest of my life at sea. And when I die, I'll die at sea. You want to know how? I'll die from an unwashed grape...I'll die holding hands with a young beautiful doctor with blue eyes...poor lady, they'll say...the quinine didn't help...that unwashed grape took her soul to heaven..." Blanche said.

"I had a vision that I was praying. But the sister said I had to prove that everything I felt is real, not a product of my imagination..." continued Mary.

"It's time..." Yunis quietly said to Eugene.

"What's going on? Who is it? Is it for me?" Blanche said.

"It's for you, Blanche," Yunis replied.

"I'm not ready yet," said Blanche, fearful. "I'll..."

"I'll pray, and..." Mary continued.

"Did we pack everything?" Stella cried in despair.

"I didn't get my white dress!" Blanche replied.

"They're waiting," Stella said.

"Waiting? Who's waiting?" Blanche asked.

"A lady, Blanche. A lady is waiting for you. She's dressed in a very nice suit…" Stella said.

Yunis, the woman dressed in the suit, got up from the chair and approached the two women.

"Suit? Is she sweet and kind? And does she have brown hair and kind eyes?" asked Blanche as she watched Yunis approach her.

"Yes, Blanche," Stella replied.

"How do I look?" Blanche abstractedly asked.

"Beautiful…" Yunis quietly answered.

"Have you forgotten anything?" Stanley said in a repulsive voice, banging the deck of cards on the table.

"Yes…I did," Blanche replied in a broken voice. She constantly addressed Yunis as if everyone else was behind a glass window, unable to influence her.

"What did you forget, Blanche? We'll send it to you with your chest!" Stanley replied.

"I really need it…when I had it…I felt no fear…or loneliness…I can't have lost it forever…but I constantly dream and forget…" Mary said.

"Oh, let's see…powder, perfume…you've got everything, Blanche," Stanley replied.

"How could I expect you to understand? I didn't know how it happened either…I think it was when…" Mary said.

"What have I done? What have I done, Yunis?" Stella cried.

"…I realized I had lost…" Mary continued without listening to them.

"You did what you had to do, Stella. She couldn't stay there…" Yunis said.

"…my soul!" Mary said, holding Blanche's hand as if seeing her for the first time.

"We're so foolish to talk about it. It's not her fault. She doesn't hate us!" Jamie replied. He was totally lost in the game; there was almost no warmth inside him, almost nothing connecting him to his mother anymore.

"Leave it to me!" Yunis said with a reassuring voice.

The crescendo of voices and feelings that had taken a bizarre turn abruptly stopped once Yunis's watch stopped ticking. Everyone froze in their seats. Blanche started talking slowly and calmly, looking at the woman in the 'suit' in the eye and holding Mary's hand tight.

"When I die…I'll be buried at sea…my body will be thrown at the waves…Mid-day! Midsummer! In an ocean as blue as the eyes that…"

"…that entered my heart and soul…But then something happened. For a while, I was…happy," Mary added.

The two women's bodies created a figure that made them seem as one. They sat on the chest that hid inside it all of their valuable memories. After Yunis silently excused the young nurse, the room was filled with a white light produced by fluorine lamps that suddenly turned on. A sterile and neutral institution room was revealed. The cold light now covered each room that used to be lit by the color of their memories. Nothing resembled the little yellow lamps, wooden tables, and armchairs. A white light now covered everything. People and furniture. Everything seemed far away, belonging to the past. As if they only existed in an abandoned house in which everything was covered under white sheets.

Mary dropped the white wedding gown, and Blanche took off the faux tiara she wore on her head. They seemed calm and pure; their bodies were now light, nothing weighing them down. They seemed like two little girls, innocent and pure, back when their reality was nothing but white. Back when nothing was written on their life's pages and the colors of their moments had not yet appeared. Their souls' journey had found its path towards the 'door' of serenity. They put their self aside, the selves that kept them locked inside their fears and passions, and finally found what they were looking for.

"Mary…Blanche, Miss DuBois!" Yunis softly whispered in their ear, trying to wake them up from the serene torpor they were in.

They both smiled at her, reassuring her that their 'common journey' had reached its end. The young nurse opened the institution's wooden door. The blinding light covered everyone's face, as well as those sitting around the table. Everyone got up, quietly and discreetly, and stood in front of the woman in the suit, young doctor Jane. They introduced themselves by their real names. Joseph was Jamie, Nick was Edmond, Alfred was James, Net was Stanley, Peter was Mitch, and Katie was Stella. They were all inmates of an institution and had walked the same path as the two women. They, too, were trying to find their own reality, which was written from the beginning.

With Jane's permission, they looked at the two women one last time and went out through the big wooden door through which an intense light came, turning them into white, bright figures.

"Carried away by a fairytale, you waste your life looking for a magic door, a lost kingdom of serenity."

Eugene O'Neil